↑

river

South
Downs

Ben's
house

Button
found here

Sky
found here

Chicken coop

Farmyard

Jasmine's
house

Calf barn

Holly
found here

Lucky
born here

To Roger Turner's farm →

Jasmine Green Rescues
A Collie Called Sky

Read all the books in the
Jasmine Green Rescues series

Jasmine Green RESCUES
A Collie Called Sky

Helen Peters

illustrated by **Ellie Snowdon**

WALKER BOOKS

Text copyright © 2017 by Helen Peters
Illustrations copyright © 2017 by Ellie Snowdon

First US edition 2020
First published by Nosy Crow (UK) 2017

Library of Congress Catalog Card Number pending
ISBN 978-1-5362-1026-2 ((hardcover)
ISBN 978-1-5362-1571-7 (paperback)

20 21 22 23 24 25 LBM 10 9 8 7 6 5 4 3 2 1

Printed in Melrose Park, IL, USA

This book was typeset in Bembo.
The illustrations were done in pencil with a digital wash overlay.

Walker Books US
a division of
Candlewick Press
99 Dover Street
Somerville, Massachusetts 02144

www.walkerbooksus.com

For my sister Hazel
HP

For Sarah and Daisy
ES

1

A Tiny Whimper

Jasmine and her best friend, Tom, were shoveling pig feed into a bucket when Jasmine suddenly remembered something.

"Guess what?" she said. "I'm going to be looking after two chinchillas in August."

Tom's eyes lit up. "Oh, chinchillas are so cute! Whose are they?"

Jasmine picked up the bucket. "They belong to one of the other vets at Mom's office," she said as they crossed the farmyard toward the orchard.

"They're called Clover and Daisy. They've got this huge cage that's going to go in my bedroom. I can't wait."

A large mallard drake waddled across the yard toward them, flapping his wings and quacking. Jasmine laughed as he nibbled at her boots.

"Don't be jealous, Button," she said, stroking his silky feathers. "You know you're the best duck in the whole world. And Clover and Daisy are only coming for two weeks. You're mine forever."

Tom and Jasmine had rescued Button in the spring, when he was just an orphaned egg on the riverbank. Button's name suited him because his perfectly round eyes looked like two shiny black buttons. He was a full-grown drake now, living happily with the chickens, but he still liked to follow Jasmine around the farmyard and be petted.

"Are you getting paid to look after the chinchillas?" asked Tom.

"I don't know. If I do, I'll need to give the money to Dad for Truffle's feed. She eats so much these days. But that's the whole point of having animals to board, isn't it—so that we have enough money to look after rescued animals."

The two friends were planning to set up an animal rescue and boarding center when they grew up. The idea had been inspired by Truffle, Jasmine's pet pig, who was now trotting across the orchard to greet them. She had been a tiny runt piglet on the point of death when Jasmine had smuggled her home from a neighboring farm and nursed her back to health eight months ago.

Tom tipped the feed into Truffle's trough, and Jasmine scratched her behind the ears as she gobbled the pignuts.

"When are the chinchillas coming?" asked Tom.

"Not until the middle of August. Three weeks to go."

When Tom had to go home for lunch, Jasmine walked up the farm driveway with him. Fluffy white clouds perched high in the bright-blue sky.

"The sky looks like a painting, doesn't it?" said Jasmine.

"It's better than a painting," said Tom, "because it changes all the time."

"Like a new painting every day."

In the field to the left of the driveway, Jasmine spotted her five-year-old brother, Manu, and his best friend, Ben, crouched by a clump of hawthorn bushes.

"Look what we found!" called Manu.

"Ugh," said Tom. "That's creepy."

It was an animal's skull, with big eye sockets and a complete set of teeth.

"Look, it still works," said Ben. He moved the lower jaw to make the mouth open and shut.

"It's a badger," said Manu. "We've got a leg bone, too. We're looking for the rest of it."

"I'm hungry," said Ben.

"There's cookies at home," said Manu, and they ambled back toward the house.

Jasmine said goodbye to Tom at the end of the driveway. As she turned to walk back home, a little sound made her stop. Frowning in concentration, she stood still and listened.

The air hummed with insects. Bees buzzed in the clover and butterflies fluttered among the dog roses and rosebay willow herb. In the next field, a kestrel hovered, waiting to pounce on its prey.

I must have imagined it, she thought. She started to walk on. But then she heard it again. A tiny whimper. It seemed to be coming from the hedge.

Jasmine walked back and scanned the thick

hedgerow. There was no sign of an animal. She dropped to her knees and looked underneath the hedge.

And then she saw something. A heap of matted black and white fur. Was it a dead animal? A badger, perhaps?

The heap of fur whimpered again. Jasmine moved closer so she could see it properly.

A dog! A little border collie, hardly more than a puppy, by the looks of it. But it wasn't a normal, healthy puppy. It looked barely alive. Its eyes were closed and its bones jutted out beneath the dull, matted fur.

"Hello," said Jasmine softly. "Hello, little dog. What are you doing under there?"

The puppy whimpered again, but it didn't move.

"Are you hurt?" Jasmine asked. "Are you stuck? Let me get you out of there."

She reached in and gently put her arms around the little dog. She picked it up and gasped in

shock. It was much lighter than she had expected. Its hip and shoulder bones stuck out from its body, and she could see every one of its ribs under the matted coat.

"Oh, my goodness," she said. "Oh, you poor, poor thing, you're starving!"

The puppy lay limp in Jasmine's arms, taking fast, shallow breaths. She tried to stand it up but

it just flopped down again on its side in the grass. It clearly had no strength at all in its legs. It didn't even seem to be able to lift its head up.

Jasmine looked at her watch. Her mom, who was a vet, would still be taking morning clients at the practice where she worked, four miles away. Jasmine could phone her and ask her to bring medicines and supplies, but she wouldn't be able to get back for at least an hour. Dad had gone to collect some new beef calves from a neighboring farm. Jasmine's older sister, Ella, was at home, but she wouldn't have a clue what to do with a sick puppy.

Jasmine scooped the little dog up in her arms and held it close. The puppy opened its amber eyes and looked at her, and the tip of its tail slowly began to wag. The look in its eyes was one of absolute trust.

Jasmine bent down and kissed the top of its head.

 8

"Don't worry, little dog," she said. "I'm going to take you home and make you better. You'll be all right now. I promise."

2

What Have You Brought Home Now?

Jasmine's heart was beating very fast as she walked home, cradling the dog in her arms. After that one sign of life, the puppy had closed its eyes again and had made no further movement. Jasmine had seen enough sick animals to know that, despite her reassurances, the little dog was very close to death.

The farmhouse was silent as she opened the front door and walked into the hall. There was an empty cookie tin on the kitchen table. Manu and Ben must have eaten all the cookies and gone out again.

Cradling the silent, unmoving puppy, Jasmine grabbed a pile of clean towels from the linen closet and put them on the kitchen table. Then she carefully laid the dog on its side on the towels.

It was a horrifying sight. The little dog, whom she now saw was a boy, was barely more than a skeleton covered with a thin layer of skin and tangled, dirty fur. There were bare patches and sores on his skin where the fur had rubbed off in places, and he also had sores under his tail.

Jasmine took a deep breath. *You need to calm down and think like a vet,* she told herself. *You've spent enough time watching Mom at work. What would Mom do now?*

If the dog was starving, he was probably also dehydrated. Gently, she pinched the skin on his neck, as she had seen Mom do. Instead of springing back when she let go, like normal, healthy skin would, it stayed puckered up. The dog was

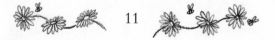

extremely dehydrated. She needed to get some liquid into him.

She found a clean dog bowl in the mudroom, filled it with water, and carried it carefully to the table. She set it beside the dog, but he didn't move. Gently, she lifted his head and slid the bowl under his mouth, still supporting his head. To her delight, he opened his eyes, put out his tongue, and started to lap the water.

"Good boy!" said Jasmine. "Good boy, you're drinking!"

She held his head until he stopped lapping and then gently laid it down again. Stroking his ear, she considered him thoughtfully. "If you can drink," she said, "then maybe you could manage to eat something, too."

Mom had special canned food for sick dogs at the office, but until she came home, the best thing to tempt the puppy would be chopped cooked chicken.

Jasmine opened the fridge. Dad often made himself a chicken sandwich for lunch. Sure enough, there was half a cooked chicken breast in a container on the middle shelf. Jasmine took it out. Dad would have to have a cheese sandwich today.

Taking a chopping board from the sideboard, she carefully cut the chicken into tiny cubes and put them on a saucer. "I don't know if you'll be able to eat," she said to the puppy, "but let's see."

She lifted his head and slid the saucer under his mouth. To her amazement, the little dog wolfed down everything, licking the saucer clean

afterward. Jasmine smiled at him as she laid his head back down.

"Well done, little one," she said, ruffling his tangled fur. "You're doing really well. I'll have to tell Nani about you when we Skype next. She lives in Kolkata."

Jasmine walked over to the sideboard, picked up the phone, and dialed the number of the vet's office where her mom worked.

"Leconfield Veterinary Practice," said the woman on the other end. Jasmine recognized the voice of Mina, one of the nurses.

"Hello, Mina," she said. "It's Jasmine. Could you give a message to my mom, please?"

"Your mom's right here," said Mina. "She's just finished with her last client. I'll hand you over."

"Hello, Jas," said Mom. "Is everything OK?"

"When you come home," said Jasmine, getting straight to the point, "could you bring an IV drip and an IV drip stand, please? And some of that special canned food for sick puppies."

There was a slight pause at the other end of the line. Then came a heavy sigh. "Oh, Jasmine," said Mom. "What have you brought home now?"

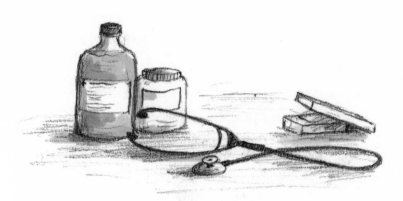

3
I Can't Let Him Down

Half an hour later, the front door opened. Jasmine hurried into the hall to meet her mother. Mom looked tense as she carried a tall IV stand and a big case full of equipment and medicine into the kitchen, but as soon as she saw the little dog lying on the table, her expression changed to one of horrified concern.

"I found him under the hedge by the road at the top of Hawthorn Field," said Jasmine. "He's a boy. I checked."

"You poor little thing," said Mom, stroking the dog's tangled coat. "What happened to you?"

"He weighs hardly anything," said Jasmine, "and he can't even stand up."

Mom went over to the sink and washed her hands. "Let's move him into the mudroom" she said, "and examine him properly. You can be my nurse, Jasmine. You can start by wiping down the mudroom surfaces. Where are the boys?"

"I don't know," said Jasmine as she took a clean cloth from the cupboard under the sink. "They ate all the cookies and went out again."

"Good," said Mom. "Hopefully they won't want lunch for a while, then. Dad can make them sandwiches when he gets back."

Mom brought the puppy on his heap of towels through to the mudroom, and laid him on the work surface. His eyes were closed and he made no attempt to move.

"He's really dehydrated," said Jasmine. "I pinched his skin and it didn't spring back."

 17

"Have you tried giving him anything to drink?" Mom asked.

"Yes, I gave him a bit of water. He can't lift his head on his own but he drank when I held his head up. And he's eaten, too."

Mom shot Jasmine a worried look. "What did you give him?"

"Some of that cooked chicken breast, chopped up really small."

"Not too much?"

"No, just half a breast."

"Good girl. We can't overfeed him. Little and often is the key. Same with water."

"That must be a good sign, though, isn't it?" said Jasmine. "If he's eating and drinking?"

Mom looked at the dog and then at Jasmine.

"I'm afraid this is a very sick dog, Jas."

Jasmine was so scared to ask the question that she could hardly breathe, but she had to know the answer.

"Will he survive?" she asked.

Mom paused. "To be honest," she said eventually, "I don't think he has much of a chance. The problem is, his internal organs have been put under so much pressure from the starvation that he could suffer from organ failure at any time. We'll do our best, of course. But you have to understand, Jasmine, that a dog this emaciated is unlikely to survive, and even if he does, he might have lasting damage to his organs."

"You should have seen the look he gave me when I told him I was bringing him home," said Jasmine. "And he wagged his tail. He trusts me, Mom. He trusts me to make him better. I can't let him down."

Mom stroked Jasmine's hair. "We'll do our very best. Now, let's give him a thorough examination. Go grab the bathroom scale, and get a pen and paper, too. You can make a chart to record the results."

When Jasmine returned with the scale, Mom lifted the puppy onto it.

"Nine and a quarter pounds," she said. She laid the dog back on the towels. "Write that down, Jas. You'll need to divide your paper into columns. Put the date in the first column. Then you need columns for weight, temperature, pulse, treatment, drugs, and feeding. You can fill the details in every day."

While Mom got the equipment ready, Jasmine divided the sheet of paper into seven columns

and wrote a heading at the top of each. She filled in the date and then, under *Weight,* she wrote *9.25 lbs.*

"How much should he weigh?" she asked.

"I'll examine his teeth in a bit," said Mom, "to get a better idea of his age, but if he's what I figure, which is about five months old, then he should weigh three times that. He weighs less than a cat, poor little thing. Now, wash your hands and then you can help me with the IV."

Jasmine had seen Mom setting up an IV before, but this was the first time she had been the head nurse. She held the little dog and talked softly to him as Mom shaved the hair from his right foreleg and cleaned the area with antiseptic. She held the catheter in place while Mom taped it to the dog's leg and attached the fluid line.

"Since he's drinking," said Mom, "he should only need to be on the drip for a few hours. It will just help to rehydrate him and get some nutrients into him."

"I won't leave you," Jasmine said to the puppy, stroking his head. "I'll stay with you the whole time."

"Now we need to give him the examination," said Mom. "You can fill everything in on the chart."

First, Mom took the puppy's temperature to check for hypothermia, and then she checked him all over for bleeding and any obvious broken bones. "He seems to be all in one piece," she said, "so I don't think we'll need to x-ray him. You can dress these sores once I've examined him."

"How could anyone starve and abandon a puppy like this?" said Jasmine.

"It's hard to imagine, isn't it," said Mom. "When he's well enough to go to the office, I'll scan him for a microchip. If he's microchipped, we can trace the owner."

"You won't give him back, will you?"

"Well, that will depend. He might have run away, of course. But it looks more like a case of

neglect and abandonment. We'll report the owner to the RSPCA and they'll investigate."

"I hope they put the owner in prison for a very long time," said Jasmine.

She stood by the little dog, stroking him and talking to him, breaking off only to add notes to her chart, as Mom checked his eyes and ears for infections and gave his paws a thorough inspection. The dog lay on his side with his eyes shut, not moving an inch. Mom listened to his heart through her stethoscope and then gently palpated his tummy. Finally, she parted his lips to look at his teeth. He stayed completely still.

"I think he's about five months old," Mom said. "Poor little thing. You haven't had much of a life, have you?"

She unwrapped a new syringe from its sterile packaging. "I'm going to get a blood sample and take it to the office. It will tell us if there's any damage to his liver and kidneys."

She gave Jasmine a serious look. "Try not to get too attached to him, Jas. If he's not responding to treatment in a couple of days, I'm afraid it might be the kindest thing to put him down."

"That won't happen," said Jasmine, "because he'll be much better by then."

Mom sighed. "Well, let's hope so. It's lucky you found him when you did. He might not have survived another day in this state. He'll need a multivitamin and iron shot to give him a boost, and an antibiotic to prevent infection. Then I'll clip his coat around the sores and clean them out. You can get a bed ready for him. Use that plastic dog bed in the shed and line it with

24

newspaper and bedding. I'll buy some diapers while I'm out, too."

"Baby diapers?"

"Yes, we use them on dogs sometimes if they can't move."

Jasmine fetched the plastic dog bed from the shed and wiped it clean. Then she lined it with old newspapers and a special absorbent, padded material that vets used for sick animals' beds because it was easy to wash and dry.

"Once he's off the IV, you can give him a bath, and then he can sleep in here for now," said Mom. "You'll need to turn him regularly to avoid putting pressure on the sores. Now, I'd better go and see what havoc those boys are causing."

Left alone with the puppy, Jasmine stroked the back of his head.

"You've had a horrible time, haven't you," she said. "But from now on, everything's going to be different. I don't know what your name was

before, or if you even had a name, but I'm going to call you Sky. I'm going to look after you all the time and you're going to get better."

The little dog opened his beautiful amber eyes and looked into Jasmine's. And, very slowly, the tip of his tail began to wag.

4
Don't Look at Me Like That

Nine days later, Manu and Ben were making cupcakes at the kitchen table when Jasmine came in to find a snack. Ben was beating the eggs vigorously into the butter, scattering droplets of batter all around the kitchen. Manu was weighing the flour, clouds of white dust flying into the air as he tipped it from the bag into the scale pan.

"What would you rather have?" Manu was asking. "Eyes that, when you blink for more than a second, they take a photo of what you were looking at and the photo comes out of your mouth; or ears that, when you press them, they play any music you like; or teeth that, when you tap them with your fingers, you can play a tune, like on a piano?"

Ben sneezed into the mixing bowl. "Photo eyes," he said, wiping his nose with the back of his hand. Jasmine made a mental note not to eat any of the cupcakes.

"Me, too," said Manu. "Is it eight ounces or eighteen ounces, Ella?"

Jasmine and Manu's sixteen-year-old sister, Ella, was *officially* in charge of their baking. She was sitting at the other side of the kitchen, hunched over a pad of paper she had balanced on one knee. A large book was balanced on her other knee. She was scribbling notes on the paper, completely absorbed in the summer research project she had been given as preparation for her honors English course. Manu had to repeat his question twice before she realized someone was speaking to her.

"Eight," she said. "All the ingredients should weigh eight ounces."

"Oh," said Manu. "I thought that looked like a lot." He started scooping spoonfuls of flour back into the bag, sending more white clouds into the air.

Jasmine took two bags of chips from the snack cupboard and went back to the mudroom, closing the door behind her. Tom was kneeling on the floor next to the dog bed, stroking Sky's head. "Good boy, Sky," he was saying. "You're such a good boy, aren't you?"

Sky looked up and wagged his tail. He could move his head without help now, although he couldn't yet support himself on his legs. He was eating five or six times a day, but he was still very thin. It would be a while before he reached a normal body weight.

Jasmine took a box of dog biscuits from the cupboard above the work surface, and Tom gently lifted Sky into a sitting position. Sky couldn't do this by himself yet, but he could stay sitting up on his own once he was in position.

Jasmine held out a biscuit in the palm of her hand, slightly away from Sky's mouth. Sky stretched out his neck to gobble it up.

"Good boy," said Jasmine softly. "Good stretch-

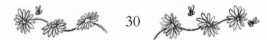

ing. Well done. Let's see if you can stretch even farther."

She laid another biscuit on the floor, slightly farther away this time. Again, Sky stretched out his neck, shot out his pink tongue, and gobbled up the biscuit.

"Good boy," said Jasmine. "You're getting stronger, aren't you?"

"Let's put him in his harness for a bit," said Tom.

Jasmine had made the harness to help Sky regain the use of his legs, after Mom had told her about similar contraptions. Sky's harness was a wide strip of terry cloth sewn into a loop and attached at the top to a piece of rope that hung from a hook Dad had fixed to the ceiling. Jasmine put Sky in it for short periods each day to help him support himself and build up his muscles.

Tom scooped Sky up and held him upright while Jasmine slipped the harness over his head and front legs. She smoothed out the fabric so that it stretched under his belly from his front legs to his back legs. Then Tom took his hands away so that Sky was in a standing position with his legs on the floor.

"I think he's putting some weight on his front legs," Jasmine said excitedly after Sky had been in the harness for a while. "Look, they're not just dangling anymore, are they? Clever boy, Sky. You're getting stronger."

At the sound of her praise, Sky looked adoringly at Jasmine and wagged his tail.

"He's so cute," said Tom. "Do you think you'll be allowed to keep him?"

Jasmine looked at Tom incredulously. It had never even crossed her mind that she wouldn't be allowed to keep Sky. "Of course I'm going to keep him," she said.

"You're so lucky," said Tom. "I wish I could have a dog."

"You can help look after Sky any time you like," said Jasmine.

Through the clattering and chattering in the kitchen, Jasmine heard Mom's car pull up outside.

"I want Mom to see Sky standing in his harness," she said, opening the door from the mudroom into the kitchen just as Mom opened the other door that led into the kitchen from the hall. Her partner at the vet's office, Dr. David, was behind her.

Mom's eyebrows shot up and her mouth dropped open. Ben and Manu fell silent as they

registered the shock on her face. They looked
sheepishly at the table, the floor, the countertop,
and then at each other. Every surface, including
their faces, was covered in dustings of flour, sprin-
klings of sugar, smears of butter, and trails of egg
white. Broken egg yolk oozed across the floor,
and there was a pattern of footprints where they
had stepped in egg and flour and walked across
the tiles.

"Where's Ella?" asked Mom.

The boys looked around vaguely. "I don't know," said Manu. "She was here."

Mom took a deep breath. "Well, go and find her and ask her to come and help you clear up this mess, right now. And take your shoes off before you go upstairs," she said as the boys headed for the door.

"Yes, Dr. Singh," said Ben as he shuffled past her. "Thank you, Dr. Singh. Sorry, Dr. Singh."

Ben was always extremely polite to adults. It meant that he got away with all kinds of outrageous behavior.

"Sorry about that," Mom said to Dr. David. "Just my son and his friend, in typical style."

Dr. David gave a polite smile. He didn't have children. And after visiting their house, Jasmine thought, he probably wouldn't want any.

"David's come to give a second opinion on a cow, so he popped in to see how Sky's doing," Mom said to Jasmine.

"Your mom says you've done a great job with

him," said Dr. David. "He was such a sad little thing when I saw him last week."

"Come and look," said Jasmine. Dr. David had last seen Sky the day after she had found him, when Mom had taken him into the office to give him his injections and a scan. She hoped he would see a real difference now.

Sky was still in his harness. Tom was kneeling on the floor beside him, stroking his back. Sky looked up and wagged his tail as Jasmine came in.

Dr. David's eyes widened. "Wow," he said. "That's remarkable. I wouldn't have recognized him."

At the sound of Dr. David's voice, Sky's tail tucked between his legs and he shrank back, baring his teeth in a low growl.

"It's all right, Sky," said Jasmine, sinking to her

knees beside the skinny little dog. "Dr. David's a vet. He won't hurt you."

She looked up at Dr. David. "He's like this every time he hears a man's voice," she said. "He's the same with Dad. We think a man must have been cruel to him."

"Poor little thing," said Dr. David softly. "The RSPCA haven't traced anyone yet?"

"No, but they're still trying," said Mom. The scan had revealed that Sky had not been microchipped, so Mom had reported the case to the RSPCA as well as the local dog warden.

Sky was relaxing slightly now as Jasmine stroked him and murmured comforting words in his ear.

"He looks so much healthier," said Dr. David, still speaking softly so as not to frighten Sky. "And his coat's much better already."

"Jasmine's bathed him and dressed his sores every day," said Mom. "And he's eating and drinking well now."

"He's starting to support his weight, too," said Jasmine. "Look, Mom, he's using his front paws."

"You're doing a wonderful job with him," said Dr. David. "I'm really impressed."

"I'll give the shelter a call," said Mom. "At this rate, he'll be ready to go there in a few weeks, if nobody claims him."

Jasmine froze. Then she stared at Mom in horror. "What are you talking about? Sky's not going to a shelter."

"He has to go eventually, Jasmine," said Mom. "Oh, don't look at me like that. You surely didn't think you were going to be able to keep him forever?"

5
I Have to Keep Him Now

Jasmine stared at her mother in outrage. "Of course I'm going to keep him," she said. "He loves me and I love him. He's already been abandoned by one owner. He's not going to be abandoned by another one."

"Jasmine, a dog is a huge amount of work," said Mom. "It won't be like Truffle or Button, where they grow up very quickly and can just live on the farm. Sky will need hours of attention every day for his whole life, and that could be fourteen years or more."

"I know that," said Jasmine. "I've read all about looking after collies."

"Then you'll know how much work they are. How are you going to manage that when you're at school all day?"

"Only from nine till three. And I bet Dad would like to have him around while I'm at school. I'm going to train him as a sheepdog when he's old enough so he'll be a help to Dad."

Dr. David was looking increasingly uncomfortable. "I'd better go and look at this cow," he said. "Where is she?"

"She's in the old bull pen," said Mom. "Michael should be around. He's probably feeding the calves. Thanks, David. And sorry about the chaos."

"Are you still going to be all right to look after the chinchillas?" Dr. David asked Jasmine. "Or will you be too busy with Sky?"

"Oh, no, I'll definitely look after the chinchillas," said Jasmine. "It's summer vacation now, so I've got plenty of time."

As soon as Dr. David had left the room, Jasmine said, "I can't believe you're thinking of sending Sky to the shelter! Do you want him to spend his life in a cage, looking out through the wire with sad, hopeful eyes like all those other poor dogs? How can you even bear to think of it?"

Jasmine's parents had taken her to visit the shelter once and had vowed never to do so again after she had begged to take home every animal in the place.

Sky started to whine.

"See?" said Jasmine. "He knows. You've upset him."

"He's upset because he can tell you're upset," said Mom.

"So don't upset me, then."

Mom raised her eyebrows warningly. "I don't think we should be having this conversation in front of Sky," she said. "Or Tom, for that matter. Sorry, Tom."

Jasmine followed her into the kitchen, which

looked marginally less chaotic than before. Ella was sitting in the corner reading her book. Manu and Ben were at the table, stirring a vast quantity of blood-colored liquid in Mom's largest mixing bowl.

"What on earth is that?" said Mom.

"Icing," said Manu. "For the cupcakes."

"But that's far too runny. And why have you made such a ridiculous amount?"

"It was a bit stiff, so we added more water," said Ben, glancing at Manu. "But my elbow got bumped and I think we might have added a bit too much."

"So then we put in all the rest of the confectioners' sugar," said Manu. "Two whole bags of it, but the icing's still runny."

"Sorry, Dr. Singh," said Ben.

Mom gave Ella an exasperated glance. "Ella, you promised you'd supervise them."

"I did," protested Ella, "but if you take your eyes

42

off them for even one second, they do things no normal human being would ever think of. Like pouring in the entire bottle of red food coloring and filling the whole bowl with water."

Mom gave a heavy sigh. "Leave that icing, boys, and go do something else. Something quiet and clean. I'll sort the icing out later."

"Let's go and put that cow's tooth we found in our collection," said Manu. He looked around the table. "Where is it?"

"In one of your pockets, probably," said Mom. "That's where I usually find things, right before they go in the washing machine. If I'm lucky, that is."

Last month, the washing machine had broken, and when the repairman had been called out, at great expense, he had found several small bones and teeth inside it.

"It's not in my pocket," said Manu. "Oh, now I remember, I took it out of my pocket and put it

44

on the table, right there, before we started making the cupcakes."

Everyone looked at the table. There was no sign of a cow's tooth. Everyone turned their gaze toward the Aga stove where the cupcakes were now baking.

Ben grinned. "It'll be a game of chance," he said. "And the prize will be a lucky cow's tooth."

Jasmine sighed impatiently. "Anyway," she said to her mother, "Sky's attached to me now, so it would be cruel to give him away."

Mom turned her attention to Jasmine. "Firstly, Jas, we still don't know what happened to him. His owner might come and claim him. So there's no point even discussing it yet."

"But his owner was cruel to him! You can't let him go back."

"We don't know that for sure. Legally, we have to wait a month before rehoming him, to give an owner time to come forward. And if he does

need to be rehomed, I'm sure there are plenty of people who would love a beautiful dog like Sky. It wouldn't be safe to have him here, with his fear of loud noises. It wouldn't be fair to expect Manu to be quiet all the time."

"It would be perfect," said Ella, "but sadly not possible in this world."

Manu looked hurt. "I can be quiet," he said. "And I want to keep Sky. Ben and me are going to train him to search out animal bones."

"You are not," said Jasmine. "I'm going to train him properly. I've already been reading about it. And Dad wants a sheepdog."

"His fear of men's voices could be a real problem, too," said Mom. "There are always people visiting the farm and walking through on the footpaths, and we can't have him lashing out and biting. We'd get in terrible trouble."

"He doesn't bite!" said Jasmine indignantly.

"He hasn't so far," said Mom, "but we don't know what he might do if he was really frightened.

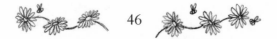

46

And what about the cats? They might not appreciate having a collie around the place."

"Jasmine!" called Tom from the mudroom. "Come and see this."

Jasmine dashed in. Sky was standing in his harness. He fixed his amber eyes on her adoringly and wagged his feathery tail.

"He's putting his weight on all four legs now, I'm sure he is," said Tom.

Jasmine crouched down and felt Sky's legs. He certainly seemed to be supporting his own weight.

"Let's take him out of the harness," she said. "Come on, Sky, we'll see if you can stand up by yourself."

She lifted the puppy up and Tom slipped the harness back over his head and front paws. Holding her breath, Jasmine gently set him down on the floor. He stood there, on his own four paws, gazing lovingly at Jasmine and swishing his tail.

Tom and Jasmine grinned at each other. "Oh,

Sky," said Jasmine. "You are the best dog in the whole world."

Mom opened the door from the kitchen.

"Look!" said Jasmine.

"Oh," said Mom softly. "That's amazing. I didn't think he'd even survive, and now he's standing up by himself."

"So," said Jasmine, "I have to keep him now, don't I?"

But Mom still wore the serious expression that meant she wasn't convinced yet. "I know he's gorgeous, Jas, and you've given him fantastic care and attention. I do know how attached you are to him, honestly. And you'll have him for a few more weeks, until he's healthy enough to go to the shelter."

Jasmine opened her mouth to protest, but Mom carried on. "All those things I said before still apply," she said. "It's a huge commitment, taking on another dog, especially a collie, and I just can't make that commitment at the moment."

6
Shut the Cage Door Carefully

Despite what Mom had said, Jasmine did not give up hope. She was certain that no owner would come forward, and her plan was to turn Sky into such a model dog over the next few weeks that the whole family would want to keep him.

The question of the cats, at least, was easily resolved. Toffee and Marmite had taken no notice of Sky at all while he was a helpless little invalid, but the first time he walked toward them on his own four feet, they crouched low to the ground and hissed so ferociously that poor Sky slunk out of the room with his tail between his legs.

"Angela says that means the cats have established their dominance over him," Jasmine told Tom two weeks later as she clipped Sky's leash to his collar and they headed down the walkway.

Angela was Tom's auntie, and she had been helping Jasmine teach Sky the basic commands of collie training. She owned a collie called Jake, whom Jasmine had looked after during spring vacation while Angela was away.

"Now she says the rest of us have to establish our dominance over him, too," said Jasmine.

"That sounds mean," said Tom.

"It's not mean; it's just because dogs are pack animals," said Jasmine. "They need to know who's pack leader. And they have to be bottom of the family pack, otherwise they won't behave. We have to show him we're always kind and fun to be with, but also that we're always in charge. And that we have all the best toys."

In the garden, they let Sky off the leash. This was as much freedom as he had been allowed so far. He still wasn't fully protected by his injections, and also he wasn't fit enough to go for long walks yet. But the big garden was a perfect place for training sessions.

Sky began to sniff about happily in the long grass. As soon as he had moved a few yards away, Jasmine called his name. He looked up inquiringly, his ears pricked. She called him again and he trotted over to her.

"Good boy!" said Jasmine, dropping to her knees and ruffling his fur. "Good dog!"

"He's learning really well, isn't he?" said Tom.

"He's good like this, with just us and nothing to distract him, but I think it will be a while before we can let him off the leash in the yard."

A flapping of wings made them both turn around, just in time to see Button flying over the low hedge and landing on the lawn. The moment Sky saw Button, he sank to the ground, his ears flattened back and his eyes fixed on the duck.

"Down!" commanded Jasmine, sweeping her arm down at the same time, palm downward. "Good boy, Sky! Good boy!" she said, crouching beside him and ruffling his coat.

"But he was already down," Tom pointed out.

"That's how you train them to understand the command. If you say it every time they begin to go down, then eventually they learn that's what they should do when you say it at other times."

She moved a few paces back from Sky. "Stay!" she commanded, her arm outstretched with the palm outward.

Sky's eyes remained fixed on Button. He began to slink toward the duck. Jasmine stepped between them.

"Stay!" she commanded again.

54

Sky continued to slink forward. Jasmine repeated the command, trying to stay calm and preparing to grab Sky if he pounced. To her great relief, Button flapped back over the hedge. Sky got up and trotted over to sniff in the flowerbed.

"Hmm," said Tom. "That one might take a while."

"That was a bit scary," said Jasmine. "It definitely wouldn't be safe to take him out on the farm yet. Not with all the chickens around."

"Let's see if he can play a finding game, like Truffle used to," suggested Tom.

"Oh, yes," said Jasmine. "If I go and hide behind a tree, he'll probably follow me anyway, so while I'm going off and hiding, you say, 'Find Jasmine!' all the time, and then when he gets to me, I'll praise him. If we do that a few times, he should get the hang of what he's supposed to do."

Sky followed Jasmine everywhere like a shadow, so he naturally followed her when she went to hide. Once they had done it several times, with

Tom calling out the command repeatedly and Jasmine praising Sky extravagantly when he reached her, Tom decided to keep Sky on the leash while Jasmine hid. When Tom let him off the leash and said, "Find Jasmine!" Sky ran to her instantly.

"Good boy!" said Jasmine. Sky rolled onto his back and Jasmine tickled his tummy while he wriggled to and fro, wagging his tail in delight.

Mom came down the walkway. "Dr. David's here with the chinchillas," she said. "Can you two help him bring their cage in?"

Jasmine, Tom, and Sky ran up the walkway. In the farmyard, Dr. David was sliding a large wire cage out of his car. It was a big car, and he had put the back seats down flat, but the cage still filled the entire space.

He looked up as they came out of the garden gate. "Hello, you two. Can you take one end of this? If it's too heavy, I'll take the branch out."

The cage had a big tree branch inside it, stretching from the solid wooden floor right to the top. Lots of smaller branches grew out from the big one.

"Where are the chinchillas?" asked Tom.

"They're in a carrying case on the front seat. We'll get the cage in place and then we can put them in it."

They took Sky to the mudroom and then helped Dr. David carry the cage upstairs. It took up most of the free space in Jasmine's room, and it reached nearly to the ceiling. Then Dr. David fetched the carrying case and placed it

on Jasmine's bedroom floor. Jasmine and Tom crouched beside it. The chinchillas were huddled in the corner. They were about the same size as guinea pigs, but they had much larger ears and bushy tails like squirrels' tails, but smaller. Their thick fur was a beautiful silvery-gray color.

Dr. David lifted them out carefully. "This is Daisy," he said, placing one chinchilla in Jasmine's arms, "and this is Clover." He handed her to Tom.

"She's so soft!" exclaimed Jasmine. "I've never felt anything so soft."

"Chinchillas have some of the softest, densest fur of any animal in the world," said Dr. David. "They have as many as two hundred thousand hairs per square inch of fur."

"Two hundred *thousand*?" said Tom, looking at Clover's mass of fine hairs. "Per square *inch*?"

"It means they never get fleas, because fleas can't get through the fur to bite them. But it also means they've been hunted nearly to extinction in the wild."

"To make fur coats?" said Jasmine, cuddling Daisy closer to her. "That's so horrible."

"Are they sisters?" asked Tom.

"Yes. Chinchillas are social animals, so it's not good for them to be kept alone. They're much happier with other chinchillas to keep them company."

"Like guinea pigs," said Tom, "and rabbits."

"Can we take them out and play with them?" asked Jasmine.

"Absolutely. Chinchillas need lots of exercise, so let them out at least once a day. Just make sure you always supervise them, and shut the cage door carefully when you put them back."

Jasmine nodded, stroking Daisy's fur. "I will. I wouldn't want the cats to get anywhere near them."

"There is that," Dr. David said, "but actually, the cats would find it hard to catch them. They're very agile and fast. They can jump up to six feet, and they're great climbers. The main problem is that they can be incredibly destructive. They gnaw anything they can get their teeth into. I let them run around my living room when I'm in there, but I've had to add chicken wire to the front of the bookcase because they started chewing the spines off my books."

Jasmine noticed a glass fishbowl on the floor next to the carrying case, filled about a quarter of the way up with a fine gray powder. "Is that their dust bath?" she asked.

"Yes," said Dr. David. "A fishbowl is good because the dust doesn't spill out too much."

Tom looked puzzled. "What's a dust bath?"

"Chinchillas can't wash in water because their fur's too dense, so they have to have a dust bath several times a week," said Jasmine. "I was watching videos online. They roll over and over in this special fine dust and it cleans their fur. It's so fun to watch."

"Well, I'm very grateful to you for looking after them," said Dr. David. He took an envelope from his pocket and handed it to Jasmine. "That's a little something for your work."

"Oh, you don't need to pay me," said Jasmine politely.

"No, I insist. Your mom says you're planning to board animals alongside your rescue center when you're older. That sounds like a very sensible business proposition to me. And it must be costing you a fair bit to keep Sky at the moment, so you can put this toward it."

"Well, if you're sure," said Jasmine. "Thank you."

"Just don't leave it lying around," said Dr. David, "or Clover and Daisy will have it. I left a twenty-dollar bill on my bedside table once and they chewed it into a thousand pieces."

Jasmine laughed and stuffed the envelope in her pocket just as her bedroom door opened and Manu came in.

"Can I see the chinchillas?" he asked. "Oh, they're so cute! Can I hold one?"

"Sure," said Dr. David, "if that's OK with Jasmine. She's in charge now."

"Be really careful," said Jasmine, "and support her properly, like this."

"It's your sixth birthday soon, isn't it, Manu?" Dr. David asked as Manu stroked Daisy. "What are you hoping to get?"

"A mobility scooter," said Manu.

Dr. David looked taken aback. "A what?"

"You know," said Manu. "One of those scooters that people who have trouble walking ride on."

"Yes, I know what a mobility scooter is," said Dr. David. "I'm just wondering why you would need one."

"I don't *need* one," explained Manu patiently. "They just look really fun."

"Right," said Dr. David. "Of course."

"Do you want one of my cupcakes?" Manu asked Dr. David.

"I wouldn't," said Jasmine, "if I were you."

"Are those the cupcakes you were making last time I was here?" asked Dr. David.

"Yes."

"Oh," said Dr. David.

"And you never know," said Manu. "If you're really lucky, you might get the one with the cow's tooth inside it."

7
Completely Ruined

"Open wide," said Jasmine to Sky, prying his jaws apart. "Good boy." She slipped the toothbrush inside his mouth.

It was a week later, and time for Sky's regular grooming session. Jasmine had brushed his coat until it shone, and now she was cleaning his teeth with a soft toothbrush dipped in a weak solution of baking soda. Sky stood still, wagging his tail gently from side to side.

"That must taste disgusting," said Tom, who

had arrived in the middle of the session. The house was quiet for once. Ella was still at a friend's house, where she had stayed the previous night. (Not that Ella ever made any noise anyway.) Ben had come by earlier, but he had gone home. Manu was up in his bedroom, Mom was at work, and Dad was out on the farm.

"It tastes revolting," said Jasmine. "I tried it. But he's very good."

"He adores you so much he'd do anything for you, that's why," said Tom. And it certainly did seem that way. Sky never left Jasmine's side if he could possibly help it.

"Time for your training, Sky," said Jasmine as she finished cleaning his teeth.

"I think he's ready for a new challenge with the finding game," said Tom.

Jasmine clipped Sky's leash to his collar. "What sort of challenge?"

"Well, he finds you every time now, just by sniffing you out. Why don't we see if he can find me?"

"OK," said Jasmine. "Let's try it."

They headed down the walkway. The weather was dull and overcast this afternoon, the sky blanketed in thick clouds. The air was still and sticky, with little black bugs flying around.

"OK, Sky," said Tom, "let's see if you can find me as well as Jasmine."

The children stood together at the top of the garden, with Sky sitting beside them. Then Jasmine unclipped Sky's leash and Tom slowly began to walk away.

"Find Tom!" commanded Jasmine, sweeping her left hand away from her in Tom's direction.

Sky looked up at her inquiringly, wagging his tail. She repeated the command. He followed her hand movement with his eyes, but he didn't move.

"Find Tom!" she said again. And this time, Sky stood up and, hesitantly at first, trotted off toward him.

"Good boy!" said Tom, crouching down and

stroking his glossy coat. "Good boy, Sky!"

Jasmine called Sky back and he bounded to her instantly. "Down!" she said, sweeping her hand downward, palm to the ground. Sky was good at this command now. He lay on the ground, his eyes fixed on Jasmine, awaiting her next instruction.

After Sky had run to Tom a few times while he was in plain view, Tom hid behind a tree while Sky was watching and Jasmine gave the command. Sky ran straight to Tom.

"Well done, Sky," said Tom, tickling his tummy as Sky rolled onto his back. "You're a very quick learner."

"Let's see if he can find you just by your scent," said Jasmine. "I'll take him around the corner and you hide."

Just then, a piercing scream came from the house. Sky shrank back, whining and trembling. The children stared up at Ella's open bedroom window, where the scream had come from. Then

they raced toward the back door. Thunder rumbled in the distance as they ran up the stairs.

Ella was sitting on the edge of her bed, her head in her hands, clutching at her hair, rocking backward and forward. She must have just come back from her friend's house

"What's happened?" asked Jasmine. "Ella, are you sick? What's wrong?"

Ella sprang off the bed. "That dog of yours, that's what's wrong! Look what he did to my work! It's completely ruined! All my notes, completely destroyed!"

"By Sky?" said Jasmine. "But how? When?"

With a shaking finger, Ella pointed at the floor behind her. Jasmine and Tom walked around to the other side of her bed. Scattered all over the carpet like confetti were hundreds of minuscule pieces of paper. Paper that, Jasmine could just about make out, had once been Ella's carefully researched, handwritten notes for her summer research project.

"That wasn't Sky," said Jasmine. "That was the chinchillas. Somebody must have left the cage door open."

Ella stared at Jasmine. Her eyes grew huge and her face turned red. Then she strode out to the landing and flung open Manu's bedroom door. Before he could resist, Ella grabbed his arm and dragged him into her room.

"Look at this!" she yelled. "Look at it! Completely ruined! The whole summer I've been working on this, and now it's totally destroyed, all because you are so completely thoughtless that you can't even shut a cage door!"

"I did shut the door," protested Manu.

"Well, you clearly didn't shut it properly, did you? You complete and utter . . ."

Ella continued to rant, but Jasmine had stopped listening. She ran into her room, just as the sky darkened and an enormous clap of thunder sounded. The door of the chinchilla cage was open, and there was no sign of Daisy or Clover. Jasmine looked inside their sleeping boxes, but they weren't there, either.

She looked up as Tom appeared in the doorway.

"Not there?" he said, and she shook her head. "Where do you think they'll be?"

"Either here or in Ella's room, I guess," said Jasmine.

"Dibs on searching in here," said Tom.

Jasmine took a deep breath and went back to Ella's room.

Ella was still alternately ranting at Manu and sobbing, while fruitlessly scrabbling around picking up tiny pieces of paper. "All that work!

Look at it! And now I'll have to do the whole thing again and I'll never get it finished by the start of school!"

"It's not my fault," Manu was saying. "I definitely shut the door. They must have opened it themselves."

"They can't open it themselves," said Jasmine. "You didn't shut it properly. And you're not even allowed to take them out of the cage when I'm not there anyway."

Ella started ranting at Manu again. Jasmine turned her back on them and began to search the room. The chinchillas must have been tired after all that chewing. They had probably curled up in a corner somewhere and gone to sleep.

Ella's room wasn't very big and Jasmine searched everywhere. She was going through all the drawers, looking under Ella's clothes, when Tom reappeared.

"Have you found them?" she asked.

"Yes, and it's so cute. Look at this."

He led the way to Jasmine's room and over to her bed. Gently, he peeled back the duvet. And there, in the middle of the bed, snuggled up together, fast asleep, were two balls of silver-gray fur.

Jasmine's face broke out in a huge smile. "Oh, they look so sweet and peaceful. I'm so glad you found them. I hadn't thought of looking in the actual bed."

"It's lucky they didn't go to sleep in Ella's bed," said Tom, "or Ella would have crushed them."

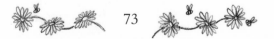

"It seems a shame to move them," said Jasmine, "but we'd better put them back."

Tom scooped Daisy into his arms. As Jasmine picked up Clover, an even louder clap of thunder sounded, followed by a dazzling flash.

"Wow, did you see that?" said Tom. "Forked lightning."

Another thunderclap crashed directly over-head, and then came the sound of raindrops drumming on the roof. As they put the chin-chillas back in their cage and Jasmine shut the door firmly behind them, her stomach suddenly turned over. In all the panic over Ella and the

chinchillas, she hadn't thought about how Sky would react to the storm.

"Where's Sky?" she said.

A worried look came over Tom's face. "Did he follow us upstairs?"

Jasmine ran to the doorway. "Sky!" she called, trying to keep the panic out of her voice. "Sky!"

There was no response.

"Sky!" she called again. "Sky!"

Still nothing.

"I'll search all the rooms upstairs," said Tom. "You do downstairs. He's probably in his bed."

Jasmine ran downstairs, calling Sky's name the whole time. She raced into the mudroom.

Sky's bed was empty. And the back door was wide open.

 75

8
One of Us Will Find Him

Jasmine felt sick. She stared through the open doorway at the pelting rain outside. She had been the last person to come through that door. She had left it open. And Sky had gotten out.

Frantically, she ran through every room downstairs, looking behind doors and furniture, under chairs, tables, and sofas, any place she could think of where a traumatized puppy might be cowering.

Tom appeared as she was making a second fruitless search of the living room.

"He's not upstairs," he said.

"Did you look under all the beds?"

"I looked under everything, behind everything, in all the closets, everywhere. Manu and Ella haven't seen him. Where could he be?"

"I left the back door open," said Jasmine miserably.

Tom's eyes grew wide with horror. "So he ran off."

"He might be miles away by now," said Jasmine. "Dogs just run and run when they're frightened. And he could have gone in any direction. Where do we even start?"

"Why don't you call your dad? He can go out in his truck around the fields. If Sky's still running, he'll probably spot him. And we can each search in a different direction. One of us will find him."

Grateful for Tom's presence of mind, Jasmine phoned her dad, who was checking the cows, and quickly explained the situation.

"He's going to drive all around the fields," she said to Tom. "And I told him you'll head up to the woods on foot and I'll go down along the river."

They grabbed their coats and tugged on their boots. Jasmine stuffed a handful of Sky's treats into her pocket and gave another handful to Tom. Then they walked out into the pelting rain.

"Don't worry," said Tom. "We'll find him."

Jasmine set off across the farmyard, calling Sky's name, trying not to let panic overwhelm her. A deafening clap of thunder made her jump. Forked lightning lit up the sky ahead.

Suddenly she had a thought so terrible that she almost threw up. What if he had run right to the edge of the farm and out onto the main road? What if a car had—

She forced herself to stop imagining such things. It wouldn't help. She just had to find him.

By the time she had opened the gate to the sheep field that ran alongside the river, Jasmine was already soaked, her clothes clinging to her skin. She walked all around the big field, calling for Sky, but there was no sign of him.

There was no sign in the next field, either. With a heavy heart, she climbed over the gate into the one beyond that. The roar of car engines and the splashing of tires were louder here. The hedge on the far side of this field bordered the main road.

And then she saw him. Running toward the road, his soaked fur clinging to his body.

"Sky!" she called. "Sky!"

But instead of coming back to her, Sky sped up. Jasmine raced after him, calling his name, but Sky just kept running. When he reached the hedge that bordered the road, he wriggled right into it.

"Stay there!" Jasmine pleaded desperately as she dashed toward him. "Stay there, Sky!"

She was almost at the hedge when, with one final push, Sky wriggled his way out of the other side and bolted onto the main road, straight into the path of an approaching car.

Jasmine raced to the gate, sick with terror. The car slowed, swerved, and drove on. Jasmine made herself look out into the road. But she saw nothing except cars driving through the rain, headlights on and windshield wipers at full speed.

And then, in the hedge on the other side of the

road, she caught a glimpse of something white among the thick green leaves.

Was it Sky? She couldn't be sure. To investigate, she would have to cross the road, something she was expressly forbidden from doing.

Jasmine looked right and left and right again, as her parents had drilled into her since she was a toddler. Only when there were no cars visible in either direction did she cross the road.

She crouched down on the wide shoulder and looked into the dense hedgerow. And there, with his back to her, howling and struggling against a bramble branch tangled in the fur on his front legs, was Sky. He was trying to wriggle out of the other side of the hedge.

Jasmine let out her breath in an enormous sigh of relief.

"Oh, Sky!" she said. "I'm so glad you're safe!"

Sky kept struggling. Jasmine climbed over the gate into the field and crouched down in front of the hedge on the other side, facing the terrified dog.

"Hello, Sky," she said. "Look, it's me. You're safe now. I've come to get you."

But Sky didn't even seem to recognize her. He just carried on yelping and struggling.

"It's OK, Sky, it's me. Let me get those nasty brambles off you."

Jasmine reached through a gap in the hedge. At that moment, a massive clap of thunder sounded and lightning tore the sky in two. And Sky sank his sharp teeth hard into her hand.

"Ow!" she cried, snatching her hand away.

Tears of shock filled her eyes. She looked at her hand.

There were four bleeding bite marks on it.

9
I Need to Get You Home

Jasmine sat by the hedge in shock. She couldn't believe what had happened. It had never, ever occurred to her that Sky might bite her.

For some time, she just sat, nursing her sore hand, unable to think straight. Eventually, though, she made herself get her thoughts in order and remember some of the things she had read in her book on collies.

It's because he's frightened, she told herself. *That's all it is. He's not an aggressive dog. He hasn't turned wild. He doesn't fear me or hate me. He's just terrified of the storm.*

She tried to remember the section in her book about "calming signals" that humans could use to calm stressed or troubled dogs. Canine behavior experts had learned these signals from watching the body language that dogs used to calm each other in tense situations.

Jasmine got up from the soaking ground and pushed away the hair that was plastered to her face. Sky was still yelping and whimpering in the hedge. Trying to remember the right signals from the book, Jasmine bent over in a play bow, with her arms stretching down in the way a dog would stretch its front legs. Then she sat down again, fairly close to Sky, but with her body turned sideways from him. This would avoid eye contact, which, in his current state, he might see as a threat. She gave a big yawn, to signal that she wasn't being aggressive, and licked the sides of her mouth. Dogs lick their noses, but Jasmine couldn't quite manage that.

84

Was it just wishful thinking, or were his yelps becoming less frantic?

Jasmine gave another yawn. Then she lowered her face and sniffed the ground. Finally, she stretched out and lay facedown on the drenched grass. She was so cold and wet by now that it wouldn't make any difference.

She lay there until Sky had stopped yelping and his cries had quieted to a whimper. She risked a sideways glance at him. He seemed to be trying to reach her. To free him, though, she was going to have to reach into the hedge and disentangle him from the bramble. Would he trust her this time, or would he bite her again?

Slowly, she raised herself to a sitting position, yawning and licking around her mouth to reassure him that she wasn't being aggressive. She remembered the packet of dog treats in her pocket. That might help.

She ripped open the bag with her teeth and put a few treats in her left hand. Her right hand

was too sore to use. Then, still avoiding eye contact, she stretched her arm very slowly through the gap in the hedge.

Holding her breath, and desperately hoping there wouldn't be another clap of thunder to spook Sky, Jasmine dropped the dog treats on the ground where he could reach them and then began to work the brambles out of his coat, yawning and licking the sides of her mouth as she did so.

To her great relief, Sky stretched his neck forward and gobbled up the treats.

"Good boy," said Jasmine softly. "Good boy, Sky, well done."

She carried on gently disentangling the brambles. He gave a little yelp when she tugged a bit too hard, but apart from that, he was quiet. Finally, Jasmine was able to pull the brambles away, and he was free. She withdrew her hand and sat on the grass again.

Some instinct told her not to call him this time. When she had called him in the field, he had just run away even faster. So she placed the remaining treats in a line from Sky to herself and then sat on the ground, shivering in her saturated clothes, waiting and hoping. The rain slowed to a drizzle, and a glimmer of blue appeared through the clouds.

After a while, she heard Sky move. She glanced sideways and saw that he had stood up. She forced herself to sit still and wait, yawning now to calm herself as much as Sky.

Hesitantly, Sky edged forward. He was still wearing his leash, but Jasmine resisted the temptation to grab it in case that panicked him again. She continued to wait.

Sky edged closer and closer until she could feel the warmth of his breath. And then she felt something that made her heart soar with happiness: Sky's little tongue licking her hand.

"Hello, Sky," she said softly. "Hello, boy. Everything's all right now. Everything's all right."

She wanted to pick him up and cuddle him, but she made herself stay still until she was completely

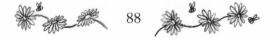

sure he trusted her again. A huge smile spread across her face as he wriggled into her lap, lifted his head, and licked her neck.

"Good boy," she said, finally allowing herself to stroke his back. "Good boy, Sky."

Sky snuggled into her lap and licked her face. For a while, she just cuddled him, reveling in the feeling of having him safely back. Then she said, "I need to get you home, Sky. Everyone is worried about you."

Holding tightly to his leash, Jasmine lifted Sky gently off her lap. Then, stiff from the cold and from sitting motionless on the hard, wet ground, she got to her feet and set off for home.

10
What Happened to Your Hand?

When Jasmine got home, the house was empty. She phoned her dad, who was very relieved to hear the news. It turned out that not only Tom, but Manu, and even Ella, were out looking for Sky.

"I'll round up the others in the truck," Dad said, "and we'll be back as soon as we can."

Jasmine took the shivering dog out to the mud-room and wrapped him in an old towel. She gave him food and water, rubbed him dry, and brushed his coat. When the key turned in the front door, she assumed it was Dad with the others, so she was surprised when her mother walked into the mudroom.

"Oh, Jasmine," she said, "you're absolutely drenched. Are you all right?"

"I'm fine," said Jasmine. "It was Sky who wasn't."

"I just got Dad's messages," said Mom. "I was in surgery. Any injuries?"

"No, thank goodness," said Jasmine as she finished brushing Sky's coat. "He was caught in brambles, but only his fur. He walked home with me and I think he's fine, except he must be really tired."

"To your bed, Sky," said Mom, pointing to Sky's spot. He walked over and curled right up in his bed.

"He should sleep well," said Mom. "It's you I'm worried about. You look absolutely frozen. Take those wet clothes off and let's get you in the bath."

After her bath, Jasmine went down to the kitchen in her pajamas and robe. Mom made hot chocolate and toasted tea cakes.

"Dad's just taking Tom home," she said, "and then he'll be back with the others."

She slid a mug of hot chocolate across the table. Jasmine stretched out her hand to take it. Mom frowned.

"What happened to your hand?"

Jasmine pulled it back. "Oh, I just caught it on the brambles."

"Let me see."

"It's fine, honestly."

"Jasmine, show me your hand," said Mom in her sternest voice.

With a twisting knot in her stomach, Jasmine held her hand out.

Mom looked at her in horror. "Sky *bit* you?"

Tears filled Jasmine's eyes. She tried to blink them back. "He didn't mean to. He was frightened of the thunder. It was all my fault."

Every muscle in her body was tense, waiting for Mom to say, "I warned you this might happen. It's not safe. We can't keep him here any longer."

But instead, Mom said gently, "Tell me all about it."

So while Mom cleaned the bite wounds, Jasmine told her everything. The only thing she left out was the fact that Sky, and therefore she, had crossed the main road. This part, she felt, was

not essential to the story and would only cause unnecessary fuss.

When she had finished, she waited with bated breath for Mom's verdict. Mom was silent for a nerve-rackingly long time. Finally, she said, "We're lucky that Sky is vaccinated—you know how serious dog bites can be in India. The good news is, once he had bitten you, you did all the right things. It was lucky you'd read about calming signals. It sounds as though you used them very effectively."

She paused. Jasmine stayed tense and expectant. Mom clearly had more to say.

"Your mistakes were all in the buildup to the bite," said Mom. "Sky didn't want to hurt you. He loves you more than anything. But at that point, he was simply acting from his deepest instincts. Your big mistake, apart from leaving the door open in the first place, was to call him back when you went looking for him."

Jasmine stared at her. "What do you mean? How else would he come back?"

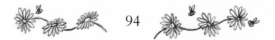

"I know it goes against all your instincts," said Mom, "but the one thing you really shouldn't do with a dog that's run off in fear is call it. The noise that spooked him brought out his fight-or-flight response, you see, and a dog's instinct in that situation is just to run and run, to get as far away as possible from the perceived danger. If you call him back, he just keeps on running, because his instincts tell him not to allow himself to be caught."

"So what should I have done?" asked Jasmine.

"Well, when you saw him," said Mom, "you should have kept a bit of distance and used the calming signals, so that, eventually, he would settle down and come to you. When you put your hand in the hedge to try to catch him, he was so panicked that he probably didn't even recognize you. He just saw you as another threat. And it was particularly unfortunate that there happened to be a thunderclap at that moment. Dogs have such sensitive hearing that thunder must sound absolutely terrifying to them."

"You're not going to send him away because he bit me, are you?" said Jasmine. "You know he didn't mean to. And he won't do it again. I'm sure he won't."

"There's no point even discussing it at the moment," said Mom. "It hasn't been a month since we reported him to the dog warden. Somebody still might come forward and claim him."

"Nobody's going to claim him," said Jasmine. "They left him in a hedge to die. You're just saying that because you don't want to talk about it."

"You're right," said Mom. "I don't want to talk about it. I just want to make dinner in peace."

Jasmine went to her room, tired but very relieved. Mom hadn't said she would send Sky away, and Jasmine was sure that nobody would claim him now. There were only four days left until the month was up. And then Sky would be hers forever.

 96

11
She Can't Take Sky Away

Three days later, Jasmine, Tom, and Sky were
playing hide-and-seek. Jasmine held Sky on his
leash around the corner of the house, where
Mom was weeding the flowerbed, while Tom
went to hide in the orchard. Sky was getting to
be a very good seeker, so they were hiding farther
and farther away.

Jasmine gave Tom a couple of minutes to hide,
and then she unclipped Sky's leash and said, "Find
Tom!"

Sky trotted off happily, his nose to the ground and his tail wagging. Jasmine followed at a distance. Tom was crouched behind a patch of nettles in the far corner of the orchard, and Sky found him easily. While Tom was praising him, Jasmine petted Truffle, who was digging up the grass under an apple tree with her tough snout. The huge sow grunted contentedly as Jasmine scratched her behind the ears.

"It will soon be autumn, Truffle," said Jasmine, looking up at the enormous old oak tree in the corner of the orchard. "And you'll have all those acorns to feast on."

"Do you want to hide?" asked Tom. "Or should I go again?"

"You hide one more time," said Jasmine, "and then let's go to the den."

Yesterday, she and Tom had started building a den in the thicket at the bottom of the horse paddock. (There were no horses in the horse paddock now, but the field had gotten its name in the days before tractors were invented, when the farm horses used to graze there.)

Jasmine gave Truffle a final scratch behind the ears and then called Sky. He started to run in front of her as they headed for the gate, and she gave the command she had learned from Tom's auntie Angela. "Stay close!"

Sky turned and came back to her immediately. "Good boy," she said. "Good boy, Sky."

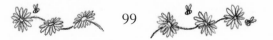

At the orchard gate, she made sure Sky stayed behind her so that she could go through the gate first. Angela had told her that this was really important.

"Always remember that dogs are pack animals," Angela had said. "They're always looking to move up the pecking order. When they try to push past you in gateways, it's because they're trying to be top dog. It's really important that you don't let them get away with it. You must always be top dog. And Sky will want to please you, so if you're consistent, he'll quickly learn what he needs to do to earn your praise."

Sky certainly wanted to please Jasmine, and he was also a quick learner. Jasmine had read that border collies are the most intelligent dogs in the world, and Sky, she was sure, was one of the most intelligent border collies of them all. She couldn't wait until he was a few months older and she could start training him to work sheep.

Mom's phone started to ring as Jasmine came

around the corner. Her mother pulled off her gardening gloves and fished it out of her back pocket. She glanced at the screen before answering.

"Hello, Linda, what's up?"

Linda was the head nurse at Mom's office. Mom listened for a minute and then said, "Are you sure she means Sky?"

Linda said something else. "Uh-huh," said Mom, nodding and listening intently. Linda spoke for what felt like ages. Mom shot a glance at Jasmine, who was standing rigid, staring at her.

"Yes, yes, I'll come in," Mom said, standing up and brushing debris off her jeans. "Give her a cup of tea and tell her I'll be there in twenty minutes."

"What was that?" asked Jasmine as Mom ended the call. "What was Linda saying about Sky?"

Mom took a deep breath.

"A woman has just come into the office. She says she's the sister of Sky's owner."

Jasmine stared at her in horror. "No. It can't be

 101

Sky. It could be any collie. Why does she think it's Sky?"

"She's brought in photos of a puppy that she says belonged to her brother. And Linda says the dog has exactly the same markings as Sky."

"No," said Jasmine. "It's not Sky. Lots of collies have those markings. She's got no proof."

"Well, that's why I'm going in now. To have a look at these photos and get more details from her."

"I'm coming, too," said Jasmine. "She can't have him. She can't take Sky away."

Mom walked over and put her hands on Jasmine's shoulders.

"I'm sorry, Jas, but I can't take you with me."

"But I have to come!"

Mom shook her head. "This could be a tricky situation and it has to be handled professionally. I need to go on my own."

"But I have to be there. Sky is my dog!"

Mom opened her mouth as though she was about to say something and then closed it again.

102

Jasmine stared at her. She knew what Mom had been about to say: Sky wasn't her dog. Sky had another owner, and that owner was about to claim him back.

"Jasmine, what are you doing?" called Tom, walking toward her. "I've been waiting ages."

Jasmine turned her back on her mother. "Let's go to the den," she said to Tom. "And afterward, let's go to your house. I'm not coming back here again."

12
It Doesn't Make Sense

Jasmine was almost speechless with anger as she and Tom walked across the horse paddock with Sky.

"How could she?" she said. "She's a traitor, going to see this woman. And she wouldn't even let me go with her. I've got a right to go. I'm the one who's been looking after Sky all this time."

"Why would an owner wait nearly a month after their dog had disappeared before they looked for it?" said Tom. "It doesn't make sense. I bet her brother isn't really the owner. I bet she just wants to get a dog for free and she's gone around to all the vets, asking if they've had any stray collies brought in until she found one that had."

Jasmine gazed at him, openmouthed. "Yes!" she said. "Of course! And that's why she's pretending to be the owner's sister, not the owner. Because then it won't look so suspicious if she can't answer all the questions."

"But even if her brother is Sky's owner," said Tom, "they won't give Sky back to him, will they? He left him in a hedge to die."

"Exactly," said Jasmine. But then a thought struck her. A thought so terrible that she stopped dead in her tracks. Sky pulled on the leash, trying to keep on walking, and Jasmine automatically gave the command, "Stay close!" Sky turned and looked at her inquiringly, and then moved back to stand beside her.

"What?" asked Tom. "What's wrong?"

"What if his owner didn't leave him to die?" said

105

Jasmine. "What if there was a storm, or fireworks, or something else that spooked him, and he ran off and got caught in the hedge and couldn't get free, exactly like the other day? What if his owner really loved him and he's been searching for him ever since?" A huge lump rose in her throat so that she could hardly speak. "I thought he was my dog, but what if he's not? What if he had another owner who loved him and has been missing him all this time?"

The lump in her throat was so big by now that she couldn't speak anymore. She quickened her pace, Sky trotting beside her. Tom walked beside her, too, and he didn't say anything. *That's because he knows I'm right,* thought Jasmine, *and there's nothing he can say to make me feel better. Sky is going to be taken away from me, and there's nothing anyone can do about it.*

At the end of the field, they climbed over the gate and Tom headed toward their den.

"Do you mind if we don't go to the den?" said

Jasmine. "I don't really feel like it today. Can we just keep walking?"

"Sure," said Tom, and they carried on toward the woods.

After a minute, Tom said, "I don't think that's right."

"What's not right?"

"What you said about Sky running off from his last owner and getting stuck in that hedge."

"Why don't you think it's right?"

"Well, Sky wasn't stuck when you found him, was he?"

"No," said Jasmine. "But he could have wriggled free eventually, and then been too weak by that time to get out of the hedge."

Tom pushed out his bottom lip thoughtfully. "Maybe," he said. "Did it look like he'd been there a long time? Was the ground all bare around him? Did it look like a dog had been frantically trying to get free for ages?"

Jasmine pictured the scene in her mind. The tiny

107

little puppy in the hedge, whimpering for help.

"No," she said. "I don't think so. I don't remember the ground being bare. And also," she said, her eyes growing large as she looked at Tom, "it would have been really smelly if he'd been there for ages, wouldn't it? If he'd been using it as a toilet all that time?"

"Really smelly," agreed Tom.

"And it wasn't. I mean, it was a *bit* smelly—*he* was a bit smelly, poor thing—but not like he'd been there for long enough to turn a healthy dog into a starving one."

"And also," said Tom, "if he'd been there all that time, I bet someone would have found him earlier. I mean, you heard him whining, didn't you? And he was quite near the road."

"And that road's a public footpath," said Jasmine. "Lots of people use it. Dog walkers. I bet another dog would have found him and alerted their owner."

"Exactly," said Tom. "So I don't believe he got stuck there. I think he was already starving, and someone just left him there to die."

"But how can we prove that?" asked Jasmine. "What if these people are really good liars and Mom believes them?"

"They must need to have proof," said Tom. "And why would anybody want a dog back if they'd thrown it out in the first place? I don't get it. Maybe," he said, turning to Jasmine, "maybe this woman wants to report her brother for cruelty, and that's why she got in touch."

"Maybe," said Jasmine doubtfully. "But then why didn't she just phone the RSPCA?"

Tom shrugged. "I don't know."

They walked around the woods for a while, but it wasn't a happy walk. Sky seemed to be able to sense that something wasn't right with Jasmine and he stayed very close, glancing at her frequently.

After a while, Tom's phone beeped in his pocket. He looked at the message.

"I have to go home for dinner," he said. "Are you coming?"

Jasmine thought for a moment. Then she said, "No, I'm going to keep walking for a bit. I'll go home later. But thanks anyway."

Privately, she had no intention of going home for many hours yet. She hoped her mom would get very worried about her. It would serve her right.

13
Might It Be Possible?

Once Tom had gone and Jasmine had no one to distract her, it was impossible to stop the terrible thoughts from flooding her head. What if Sky really had just run off and got stuck in that hedge? What if the owner or his sister were right now showing Mom all the photos they had taken of Sky as a much-loved puppy, photos that proved Sky was really theirs?

Or, even worse—so terrible that it gave Jasmine physical pain to think about it—what if Sky's owner had been cruel to him and starved him, but now, for some reason, he wanted him back? What if he had proof that Sky was his, and convinced Mom that he was a kind owner, but then when he got him back he planned to shut him up and starve him again?

Jasmine climbed the gate that led out of the woods into a field on the other side. She walked across the field, faster and faster, Sky trotting to keep up with her. She was blinded by tears and by the terrible visions in her head. She didn't know where she was going; she only knew she had to keep walking. As long as she and Sky were together, away from anyone who would try to separate them, that was all that mattered.

Suddenly her left foot, instead of landing on solid ground, sank deep into a rabbit hole. Jasmine lost her balance and crashed down, twisting her trapped ankle and falling with a thud onto the hard ground.

The pain in her ankle was so extreme that, for

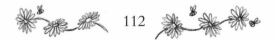

some time, she just lay on the ground, crying out and moaning. Then she felt Sky licking her nose. Still moaning in pain, she lifted her arm to stroke him. Gingerly, she heaved herself up to a sitting position so she could inspect the damage.

She was shocked to see that her ankle was already swollen. Was it broken? If she had broken it, how could she care for Sky?

The ankle hurt even more when she touched it. The swelling was hurting her foot, so, very carefully, she unlaced her sneaker and took it off, wincing as every movement sent fresh pain shooting through her body. She had no strength left to take off her sock. She just sat on the ground, moaning in pain, with Sky licking her face and hands, trying, she was sure, to make her feel better.

"You're such a good dog," she said. "And you do make me feel better. You really do."

Slowly and carefully, she shifted all her weight onto her right side and, using her hands to push herself upright, tried to stand. Eventually she managed to get herself up, but as soon as she tried to put any weight on her injured ankle, it hurt so much she almost threw up. How was she going to get home?

If she had still been in the woods, she might have been within reach of a makeshift crutch, but

here, there wasn't a stick in sight. She was well and truly stranded. And she couldn't stand on one leg for much longer.

Placing her hands on the ground, she carefully lowered herself back to a sitting position.

How long would it be before they came looking for her?

She had told her mom she was going to Tom's. Nobody would be expecting her at home for hours. And she had told Tom she was going home, so he wouldn't be expecting her at all. Even when they did start searching, it might be hours before they found her. And rain clouds were gathering in the sky.

Sky licked her face. And suddenly Jasmine had a thought.

What if . . . ?

Might it be possible? Might Sky be able to find Tom?

It would be much more of a challenge than any

game of hide-and-seek they had played before. Sky would have to go back to the woods before he could even pick up Tom's scent.

Would he do this on his own? And if he did get to the woods, he would have to trace the scent all the way through the woods and across a big field to Tom's house. Luckily, there were no roads to cross, but still, it was a long way for Sky. And if he reached Tom's house, how would he let Tom know he was there? Jasmine couldn't bear to think of Sky sitting patiently outside the house for hours, alone and unnoticed.

Sky gave a little bark and made an impatient movement.

"You want me to get up and walk, don't you?" said Jasmine. "But I can't walk."

Sky circled her, nose to the ground, tail wagging. He looked as though he had plenty of energy.

"Would you like to do a job for me, Sky?"

Sky licked her face again.

 116

Jasmine made up her mind.

"Lie down," she commanded.

Sky didn't even need the hand signal anymore. He lay on the ground, fully alert, his tail sweeping across the grass from side to side, his eyes completely focused on Jasmine's face, awaiting his next instruction. Jasmine removed his leash.

"Find Tom," she said, sweeping her hand away toward the woods. "Find Tom!"

Sky sprang to his feet. He trotted off toward the woods, sniffing at the ground. Then he turned to look back at Jasmine.

"Find Tom!" she called, sweeping her hand away again. "Find Tom!"

Sky put his nose back to the ground and continued across the field. At the gate that led into the woods, where Jasmine and Tom had parted, he started to wag his tail and sniff excitedly at the grass.

"You've found Tom's scent," said Jasmine. "Good dog, Sky."

She said this very quietly, so as not to distract him from his task. She didn't want him to think he'd completed the job already.

Sky slipped under the gate and trotted off into

the woods. Jasmine watched him until she could no longer see him through the trees.

Once he was out of sight, she felt acutely alone. Without Sky to focus on, the throbbing pain in her ankle was much harder to bear. She lay on the ground and looked up at the heavy gray clouds amassing above her. There was nothing more she could do. Exhaustion overwhelmed her and she closed her eyes.

Jasmine woke up, stiff and aching, on the cold, hard ground. It was getting dark. Her ankle throbbed. Slowly and painstakingly, she maneuvered herself into a sitting position. A vast purple bruise now covered her swollen ankle. How long had she been asleep?

Were those voices in the distance, or was she imagining them?

She heard light footsteps running through the grass, and the panting of a dog. She turned to see Sky bounding across the field toward her, barking joyfully. Behind him, at the edge of the woods, was Tom.

14
What's Going to Happen to Sky?

While they were waiting for Dad to arrive in the truck, Tom told Jasmine what had happened. He had been up in his bedroom when he'd heard a scrabbling and whining at the front door. He had opened the door to find Sky on the step.

"At first," he said, "I thought you'd changed your mind and decided to come to my house after all. I called you, but you didn't come, so I thought you must have sent Sky ahead to find me. So I told him to find you, and he just kept going back through the woods. I couldn't believe you'd have sent him all that way, so I kept stopping and calling you. But Sky never stopped. He just kept on going, and he led me right here. He was amazing."

"He's an amazing dog," said Jasmine. "Aren't you, Sky?"

Dad took Jasmine to the hospital, where she was very relieved to discover that she had no broken bones, just a nasty sprain. She was told to get plenty of rest and treat her ankle with ice for three days. She couldn't put weight on it for a week. And she was given crutches, which made the situation seem a lot more fun.

"I think we'd better get you a phone of your own," said Dad as they drove home. Seeing the look of delight on Jasmine's face, he hastily said, "Nothing fancy, just a basic one, so you can call us if you get into any more sticky situations."

As they drove down the farm road, Jasmine saw

Mom's car in the farmyard. She felt sick again. What had happened at the office? Was Sky about to be taken away from her?

When Jasmine walked into the house on her crutches, Manu's mouth fell open.

"You've got crutches? That is so cool. Can I try? Give them to me."

Mom came running downstairs and enfolded Jasmine in a tight hug. "Oh, my goodness, Jasmine, what are we going to do with you? Come into the living room and put your feet up, and I'll get some ice for your poor ankle."

"Dad's getting the ice," said Jasmine. "What did the woman say? Does Sky really belong to her brother? What's going to happen?"

But Mom wouldn't tell her anything until she was lying on the sofa with her left foot raised on a pillow, ice packs on her ankle, and Sky on the floor beside her. Jasmine gave Manu her crutches to play with, provided he played in another room. Ella sat at the dining table, hunched over Mom's laptop, books spread out all around her. Mom had suggested that she do her notes on a computer this time to make them more chinchilla-proof. Ella had clearly forgiven the chinchillas, though, as they were both snuggled up in her lap.

"They're just so soft," she said when Jasmine expressed her surprise. "They're very comforting animals. When they're asleep anyway."

"You must be starving, Jas," said Mom. "What would you like? Pasta? Beans on toast? I could throw together some cholar dal,"

"I'm not hungry," said Jasmine. "Just tell me about Sky."

Manu's head appeared around the door frame. "These are the best things ever," he said. "When your ankle's better, can I keep them?"

"Sure," said Jasmine. "Mom, tell me about Sky. *Please*."

Mom sat in the armchair opposite Jasmine. "Well," she said, "the woman who came into the office—Iris—*is* the sister of Sky's last owner. She brought in photos of him at two months old, and the dates she gave of his age and his disappearance matched up with our dates."

Jasmine couldn't speak. It really was going to happen. Sky was going to be taken away from her.

"Her brother bought Sky on a whim, it seems," said Mom, "as an eight-week-old puppy. Iris said he made a fuss of Sky at first—his name wasn't Sky then, of course—but the next time she visited, two months later, Sky was tied up in a shed

and looked skinny and uncared-for. She lives sixty miles away, so she doesn't see her brother very often."

"So why didn't she report him then?" asked Jasmine furiously.

"Her brother told her that the dog had been ill with worms, and that was why he was thin and sick-looking. He said he was treating him."

"And she believed him?"

"It sounds as though this man is a nasty piece of work, and I got the feeling that Iris was afraid to get on the wrong side of him. She said she phoned a few times, and he told her Sky was better. But when she came to visit today, there was no sign of him, and her brother told her he'd died. She was suspicious, and she asked which vet had been treating him. He gave her the name of my practice, so she came in on her way home to check his story. Of course, her brother had never been there, but when Iris told Linda about

127

it and showed her the photos, Linda realized that the dog must be Sky."

"Why would he get a dog," Jasmine said, "if he didn't even want to look after it?"

"Sadly," said Mom, "all too many people do. They fall in love with a cute puppy but have no idea of the hours they're going to have to spend training and looking after it, every single day for the next fifteen years. Collies suffer more than most. They're incredibly cute puppies, but they've been bred over centuries to be working dogs, not pets. They grow into extremely energetic dogs that need very careful training and *lots* of exercise. People can't cope with them, and then they blame the dog for being too demanding or badly behaved. Shelters are full of collies whose owners just didn't bother to consider what they were taking on."

The back door opened and Jasmine heard Dad taking his boots off in the mudroom.

"We phoned the RSPCA, and an inspector is

going to his house," said Mom. "He'll be prosecuted, and probably banned from keeping an animal again."

"He'd better be," said Jasmine. "He should be put in prison for life."

"He should be starved and thrown in a hedge to die," said Manu, hopping into the room on Jasmine's crutches. "I'm starving, Mom. What can I have to eat?"

"There might be some cookies left," said Mom. "But don't eat too many. Dad's going to make dinner in a minute."

Manu hopped out of the room.

"Careful," said Dad, coming into the hall. "We don't want any more sprained ankles today."

"But what's going to happen to Sky?" asked Jasmine.

Mom and Dad looked at each other.

"We've been thinking about this," said Dad. "Bramble is getting a bit old for full days of work, and I could really do with a sheepdog if I'm going to increase the flock. And Sky certainly seems to have the makings of a good working dog. So we wondered if you'd be prepared, Jasmine, to work with me to train Sky as a sheepdog."

Jasmine stared from her mom to her dad, hardly able to take this in.

"You mean . . . I can really keep him?"

"You've done very well with his training so far," said Dad, "and he's clearly smart and quick. So if you're happy to share him with me, then yes, we think it would be a good idea to keep him."

"Oh, thank you!" cried Jasmine, flinging her arms around Sky's neck. "Sky, did you hear that?"

"Yay!" cried Manu, running into the room. They all looked at him curiously.

"I didn't realize you were so eager to keep Sky," said Mom.

"Of course I am," said Manu, "but it's not that."
He brandished a half-eaten cupcake in the air.
"Look! There was one left in the tin, and it had
the lucky tooth inside it!"

131

"Excellent," said Dad. "And I'm sure we're all very happy that you were the one who found it."

Jasmine turned back to Sky. "First I rescued you," she said, "and then you rescued me. And now you're going to stay here forever. And, even better than that, Sky, you're going to do what collies love to do more than anything else in the world. You're going to be a sheepdog."

 132

Turn the page for
an interview with Jasmine and
a sneak peek of the next book in the
JASMINE GREEN RESCUES series!

A Q&A with Jasmine Green

How do I pick a dog?

There's nothing cuter than a litter of puppies, so getting to pick your own puppy makes you pretty much the luckiest person in the world! The most important thing when choosing a puppy is to see it with its mom. Don't buy a puppy from a pet store, because it might have come from a puppy mill, where the dogs are kept in poor conditions, haven't been socialized, and are often sick. If you're picking a dog from a shelter, the shelter staff will be able to help you find the right dog for you.

When you see the puppies, remember that their personalities will probably be similar to their personalities as adult dogs. So choose a puppy that is friendly and approachable, not the nervous one hiding in the corner or the naughty one who jumps out of the pen! Choose one that's plump and round, and look in its ears, nose, and mouth to check that they're clean and healthy-looking.

What advice do you have for training a dog?

The best thing is to join a training club if there's one in your area. Puppies need a lot of socialization, so introduce them to as many experiences as possible before they're twelve weeks old. They need to get used to typical household noises, too, like vacuum cleaners, washing machines, and lawn mowers, and different travel experiences like in cars and on public transit. Try to make everything fun for your puppy, and give them lots of praise and treats when they do well!

What are some good dog treats?

There are lots of training treats you can buy. Try to get good quality meat-based ones. You can also use little bits of cooked meat and cubes of cheese as treats, though not too much cheese, since it's not very healthy!

How many animals do you have now?

My oldest pets are Toffee and Marmite, my two cats. I also have a pig called Truffle, who was a tiny runt when I rescued her—so small she could fit in my pocket. Now that she's fully grown, she's enormous! I also have a mallard drake called Button. I rescued him when he was just an egg. And now I have my beautiful collie, Sky. He's very intelligent, and I can't wait to start training him as a working sheepdog. He's going to be amazing!

Jasmine Green Rescues

Rescues

A kitten
Called Holly

1
It Sounds Really Fierce

"This is perfect," said Jasmine, smiling at her best friend, Tom. "Come in, Sky, and don't make a sound. We have to keep it secret from Manu."

Jasmine's collie, Sky, wagged his tail and padded into the shed. Jasmine pulled the door shut. It was coming off its hinges, and the rotting wood dragged along the ground. It clearly hadn't been shut properly for years.

"Sit, Sky," said Jasmine, and Sky obediently sat on the dusty floor.

"I can't believe we've never been in here before," said Tom. "It will be really cozy when we've cleaned it up. Look, it's even got a window."

"We can bring out some old chairs," said Jasmine, "and find something for a table. And we can clear all the junk out."

The shed was a small brick building with a sloping roof in the garden of the farmhouse where Jasmine lived. Two rusting oil stoves stood in one corner, next to a tangled bundle of wire and a collapsed straw bale. On a rough wooden shelf sat a couple of dusty old jam jars containing screws and nails.

"Look," said Tom, "there's a mouse skeleton on the floor. Manu would love that for his collection."

"We can give it to him as a present," said Jasmine. Her six-year-old brother, Manu, kept a gruesome collection of animal bones and skulls in his bedroom. "But we won't tell him where we got it. This clubhouse is our secret."

"That shelf will be perfect for books," said Tom. "And we can put our maps of the rescue center up on the wall."

It was a Friday afternoon in late October, and they had a two-week fall break stretching out in front of them. Jasmine and Tom were planning to run an animal rescue center when they grew up, and their new clubhouse was where they were going to work out all the details.

"What should we call the club?" asked Jasmine.

"The Animal Rescue Club," said Tom.

Jasmine screwed up her nose. "Not very original." Then her eyes lit up. "Oh, but it's A.R.C. for short! Arc. Like Noah's Ark."

"Exactly," said Tom. "So it's where abandoned animals come to be safe. Like you, Sky."

He reached down to stroke Sky's silky fur, and Sky wagged his feathery tail across the floor.

Three months ago, Jasmine had found Sky abandoned and left to die in a hedge. She had nursed him back to health and now he was completely devoted to her. Jasmine and Tom had also rescued a clutch of orphaned duck eggs from the riverbank in the spring, after a dog had killed the mother duck. The surviving duckling, Button, was now a full-grown drake who lived happily with the free-range chickens. And Jasmine's very first rescue animal had been a tiny runt piglet that she had found on a neighboring farm. She had called the piglet Truffle, and the sick little runt had turned into a giant sow who lived in the orchard behind the farmhouse.

"I'm not allowed to keep any more animals," said Jasmine. "Mom and Dad made me promise that if I rescue any more, I have to rehome them."

"Will you still be able to look after my guinea pigs at Christmas?" asked Tom.

"Of course I will," said Jasmine. "Are you going to your granny's in Cornwall again?"

"Yes," said Tom. "It's going to be great. She makes the best Christmas dinner ever. And we're going to swim in the sea on Christmas morning."

"Swim in the *sea*? On Christmas Day?" said Jasmine. "Why?"

Tom was about to reply when something thudded against the door. Then came frantic scratching on the wood and an ear-piercing yowl.

The children looked at each other in alarm.

"Sounds like a cat," whispered Jasmine.

"A really angry cat," said Tom.

"Maybe it's a wild cat," said Jasmine, "and it's been living in this shed. And now we've shut the door and it can't get in."

The cat continued to yowl and scratch at the door.

"We could tame it and have it as our club mascot," said Tom. "If it's living here, it kind of belongs to the club anyway."

"That's a great idea," said Jasmine. "And I wouldn't be keeping an animal, because this is its home already."

"I wonder what it looks like," said Tom.

They tried to peer through the cracks in the door, but the gaps were too narrow and they couldn't see the cat.

"We need to let it in," said Jasmine, "if it lives here."

"We'd better stand far back," said Tom.

"I don't think it will hurt us. It's probably just confused because the door's shut."

Tom looked doubtful. "I don't know. It sounds really fierce."

"It'll be fine," said Jasmine confidently. She pushed the door open.

A shrieking bundle of gray fur shot into the shed. It hurled itself at Jasmine, hissing and spitting. She screamed and covered her face with her hands as the cat leaped up at her, scratching and biting. Jasmine screeched in pain. With a final terrific yowl, the cat sprang down and bolted out of the shed.

"Are you all right?" asked Tom, sounding shaken.

Jasmine sat heavily on the collapsing bale behind her. She looked at her hands. They had deep, red scratches all along them.

"That must really hurt," said Tom.

Jasmine clutched her hands together to try to stop the pain. "That cat really didn't want us to be here. Ow, my hands sting so much."

"You need to run them under the tap," said Tom. "Let's go inside."

Jasmine frowned. "What was that?"

"What?"

"That funny squeaking sound."

"I didn't hear anything."

"Listen," said Jasmine.

They listened. Birds tweeted in the garden. Sheep baaed in the field. From the orchard came Truffle's low, contented grunt.

"I can't hear anything," said Tom. "Let's go."

They stepped out into the sunny garden, avoiding the prickly leaves of the holly bush beside the shed. Then Jasmine heard it again: a high-pitched sound, somewhere between squeaking and mewing.

She turned to Tom. His expression showed her that he had heard it, too.

"What is it?" he whispered.

"I don't know," said Jasmine, "but there's something in there."

They crept back into the half-light of the shed. There was another squeaking sound.

"It's coming from behind that bale," said Tom.

The baler twine that had held the straw together had broken, so much of the straw had collapsed in a messy heap. The children peered over the bale into the dark corner.

Jasmine gasped in delight. "Kittens!" she whispered. "Oh, they're so cute!"

"Three of them," said Tom, grinning with excitement. "They're tiny."

The kittens were cuddled up in a deep nest of straw. One was a tabby, one was orange, and the third was black. The tabby kitten and the orange one lay still, but the black kitten was crawling over its littermates, mewing.

"They're gorgeous," said Jasmine. "I wonder how old they are."

"They can't be newborn," said Tom, "because their eyes are open."

"So they must be at least a week old. I don't think they're much older than that. They're so little."

The black kitten gave another piercing mew.

"It wants its mother," said Tom. And then he drew in his breath and looked at Jasmine in horror.

"Oh, no," said Jasmine. "That cat. She must be their mother."

"We shut her out from her kittens," said Tom. "And now we've frightened her away."

Which animals have you helped Jasmine rescue?

- ☐ A Piglet Called Truffle
- ☐ A Duckling Called Button
- ☐ A Collie Called Sky
- ☐ A kitten Called Holly
- ☐ A Lamb Called Lucky
- ☐ A Goat Called Willow

About the Creators

Helen Peters is the author of numerous books for young readers that feature heroic girls saving the day on farms. She grew up on an old-fashioned farm in England, surrounded by family, animals, and mud. Helen Peters lives in London.

Ellie Snowdon is a children's author–illustrator from a tiny village in South Wales. She received her MA in children's book illustration at Cambridge School of Art. Ellie Snowdon lives in Cambridge, England.

Truffle found
this way

Oak Tree Farm

← Willow found
this way

← To village and school

Tom's
house